God sent a plague of frogs!

Exodus 8

By..
Date......................................

A bright star
shone over Bethlehem.

Matthew 2

By..

Date......................................

God made the beautiful butterflies!

Genesis 1

By..
Date..

JESUS calmed the stormy water.

Luke 8

By...

Date...

Noah took two of each animal in the ark.

Genesis 6

By.....................................

Date.....................................

Jesus was presented in the temple.

Luke 2

By...
Date.......................................

Jesus had twelve disciples.

Matthew 10

By.....................................
Date...................................

JUDAS was paid to betray JESUS!

Luke 22

By..
Date...

the King of Egypt asked Joseph for help!

Genesis 41

By.................................
Date.................................

A man invited people he didn't know to his **Party!**

Luke 14

By......................................

Date......................................

God created animals to live in **rivers** and **seas**.

Genesis 1

By...

Date...

Jesus rose up and went to heaven.

Luke 24

By.....................................
Date.....................................

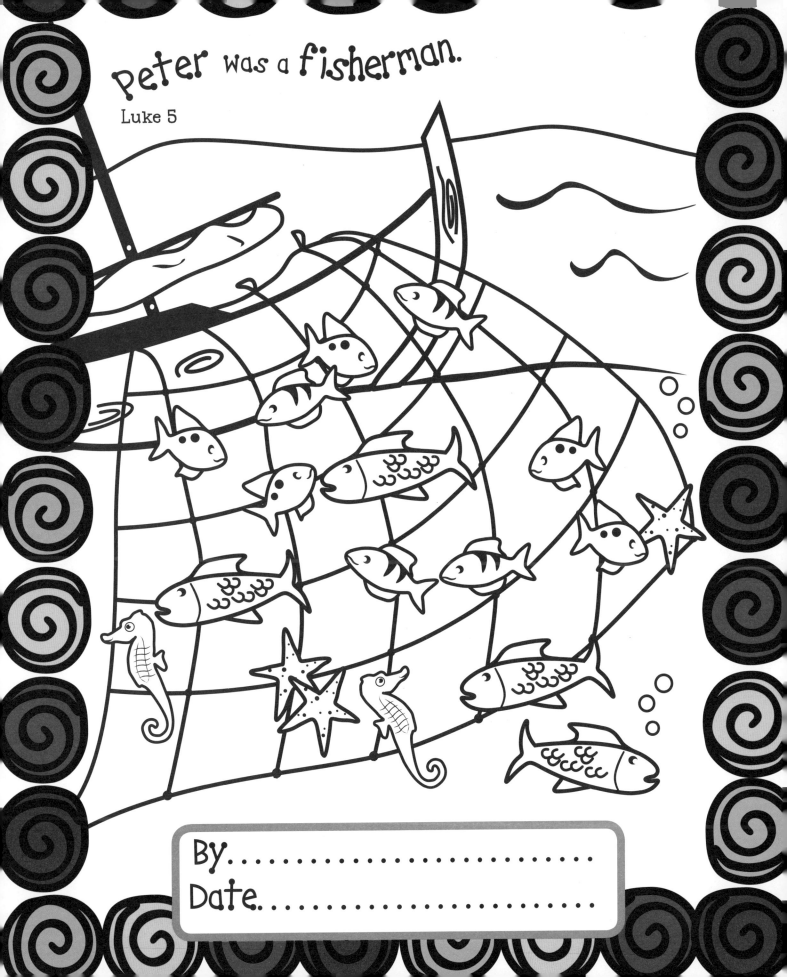

Peter was a fisherman.

Luke 5

By..
Date...

God told Jonah to go to Nineveh!

Jonah 1

By...
Date.......................................

Matthew was a tax collector.

Matthew 9

By...

Date.......................................

Joseph lived for many years in Egypt.

Genesis 41

By..

Date..

God sent a storm because he was angry with Jonah!

Jonah 1

By...
Date..

God gave Moses ten rules!

Exodus 20

By.................................
Date.................................

the kings brought gifts for Jesus!

Matthew 2

By..

Date..

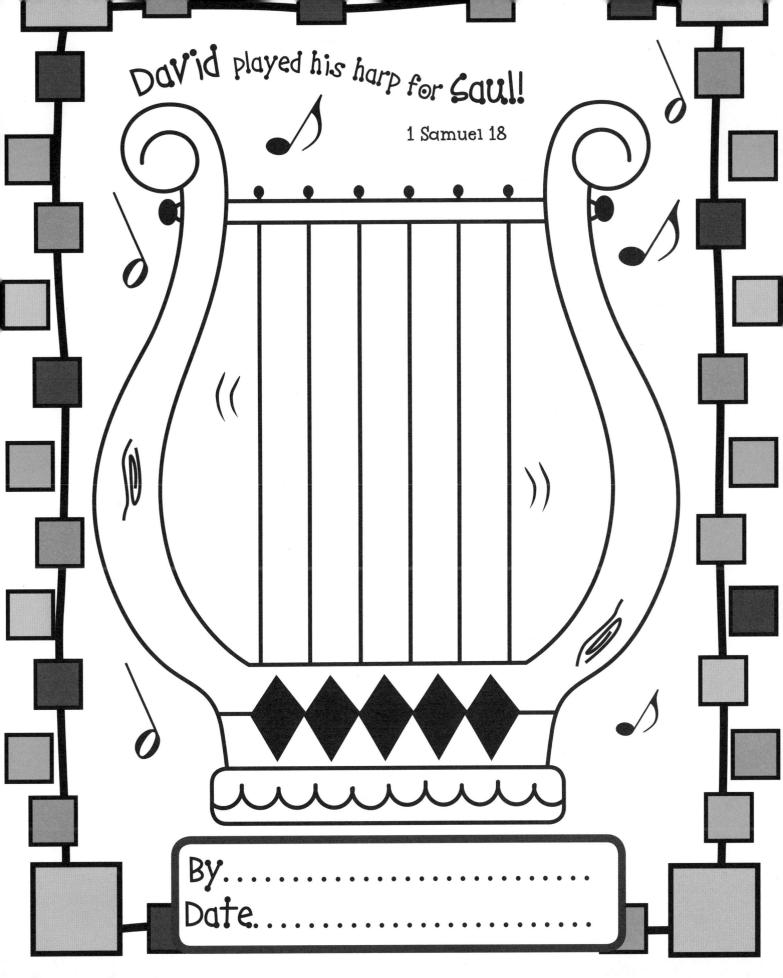

God saw all that he had made and it was very good!

Genesis 1

By...

Date...

the rain stopped after 40 days and nights!

Genesis 8

By...
Date.......................................

Samson pushed down the pillars!

Judges 16

By...
Date...

God sent ravens with food for Elijah!

1 Kings 17

By...

Date...

Jesus was born in a stable!

Luke 2

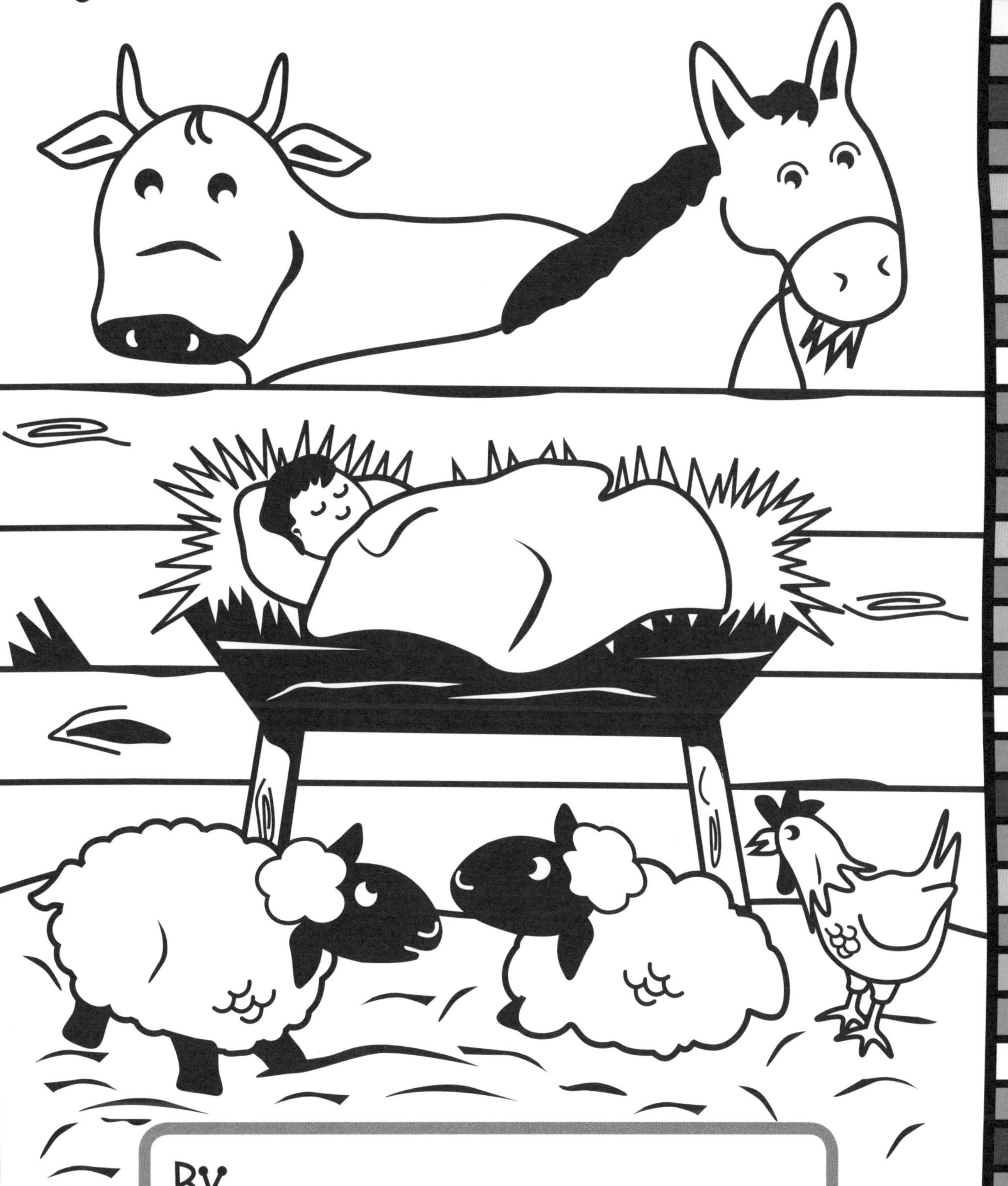

By.............................

Date.............................

Noah sent out a dove, and it came back with an olive branch!

Genesis 8

By..

Date.......................................

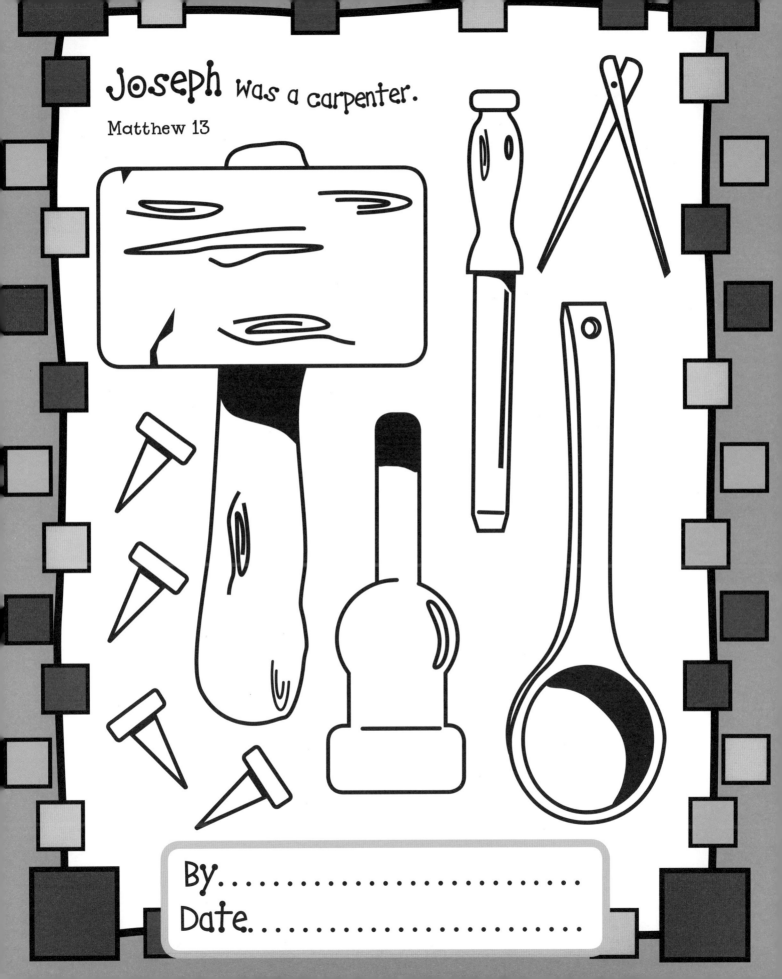

the kings followed the star to Bethlehem.

Matthew 2

By..

Date...

the spies came back from **canaan** with grapes!

Numbers 13

By..................................
Date..................................

David threw a stone at Goliath!

1 Samuel 17

By..

Date..

Roman soldiers put Jesus on the cross.

Matthew 27

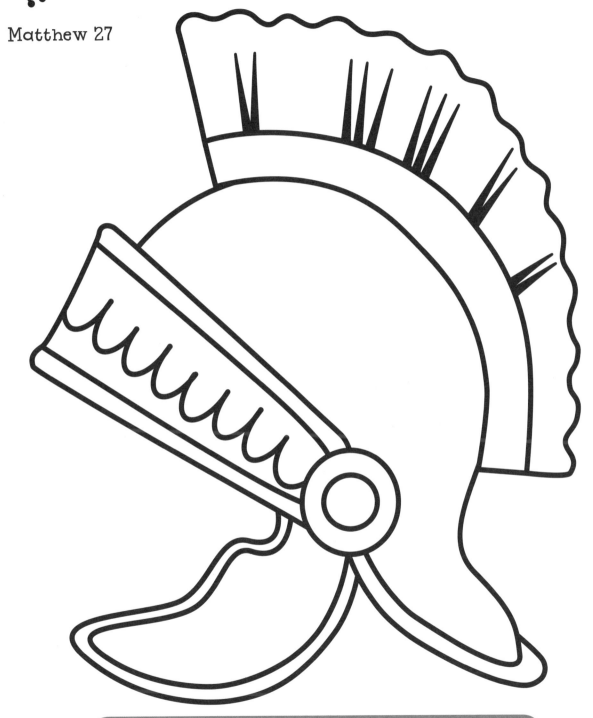

By..

Date..

the women prepared their lamps.

Matthew 25

By..

Date...

God put a beautiful rainbow in the sky.

Genesis 9

By....................................

Date..................................